For Sean-bug. Tell your dad I said you
can have a monster for a pet. —D.G.

To Marion, my favorite goblin of all time —L.T.

Text copyright © 2019 by David Goodner
Illustrations copyright © 2019 by Louis Thomas

hmhco.com

The illustrations in this book were done in gouache and pen & ink.
The text type was set in Mendoza.
The display type was set in Aunt Mildred.

Library of Congress Cataloging-in-Publication Data is on file.

ISBN: 978-0-544-76416-3

Manufactured in China
SCP 10 9 8 7 6 5 4 3 2 1
4500755782

GINNY
GOBLIN

CANNOT
HAVE A
MONSTER
FOR A
PET

Words by
David Goodner

Pictures by
Louis Thomas

HOUGHTON MIFFLIN HARCOURT
Boston   New York

Ginny Goblin loves animals.

Goats are some of her favorites.

But goats are kind of stinky, and it's
a lot of work to take care of them.

Maybe if we help Ginny Goblin
find a pet, she'll stop trying to herd
goats through the house.

But I want to be clear: Ginny Goblin should not need a giant net to find a pet. She should not need a bear trap, and she definitely should not need to drive an army tank.

Ginny Goblin cannot have a monster for a pet.

Let's take Ginny down to the beach. Maybe she'll find a tropical fish, or a cute little hermit crab. Fish and hermit crabs make excellent pets.

But, wait—where is Ginny going?

Ginny Goblin is not allowed to take a submarine to the deepest, darkest ocean depths. She is not allowed to find the great and terrible kraken.

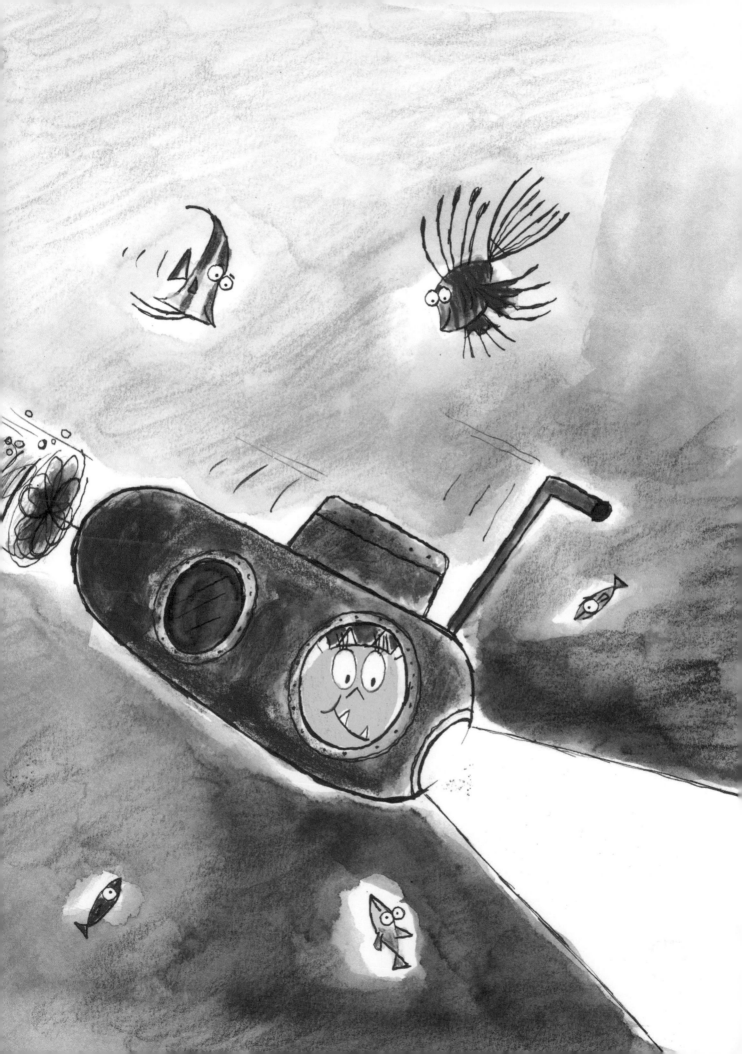

She is not allowed to put a leash on the kraken and take him home. The kraken crushes ships in his mighty tentacles, and has thousands of nasty suckers.

Krakens are unfathomable monsters, and Ginny Goblin cannot have a monster for a pet.

Ginny needs to find a pet that lives on land.

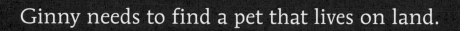

Let's take Ginny out to the hills.

Cute fluffy bunnies live in the hills.

Oh no! There Ginny goes again!

Ginny Goblin should not go into the ancient misty mountains. She certainly should not crawl down into the cold, dark cave that she finds with a magic map. She absolutely should not try to wake up a dragon and make him be her pet.

Dragons eat cows in a single bite. They burn down villages with their fiery breath! Dragons are even crankier than krakens, and they need to sleep on a bed of gold coins (often for centuries at a time).

Dragons are terrible monsters, and Ginny Goblin cannot have a monster for a pet.

Ginny needs to find a smaller pet.

Let's take Ginny to the forest. Pretty birds live in the forest, right? A little bird would be a nice pet.

A nice *safe* pet.

Ginny Goblin should not go hunting in the spooky, twisty part of the forest where all the trees are dead and the grass is scorched.

She should not make a cage trap from ropes and sticks, or bait it with cupcakes. She unequivocally should not catch a basilisk in her trap.

Basilisks live on land, and they're smaller than dragons, but they turn everything they look at into stone. If Ginny took her basilisk to school for show-and-tell, her whole class would turn into statues.

Besides, basilisks croak like big, ugly frogs, and they won't use the litter box. Basilisks are petrifying monsters, and Ginny Goblin cannot have a monster for a pet.

Ginny needs to find a pet that's not magical.

In fact, I'm starting to wonder if Ginny should have
a pet at all. Let's take Ginny to the space museum to
take her mind off pets for a while.

Oh, what now? Where is Ginny going?

Ginny Goblin is not allowed to borrow a rocket ship
from the space museum. She is completely not allowed
to ride the rocket to outer space, and if she does go to
outer space, she is not allowed to catch a space creature.

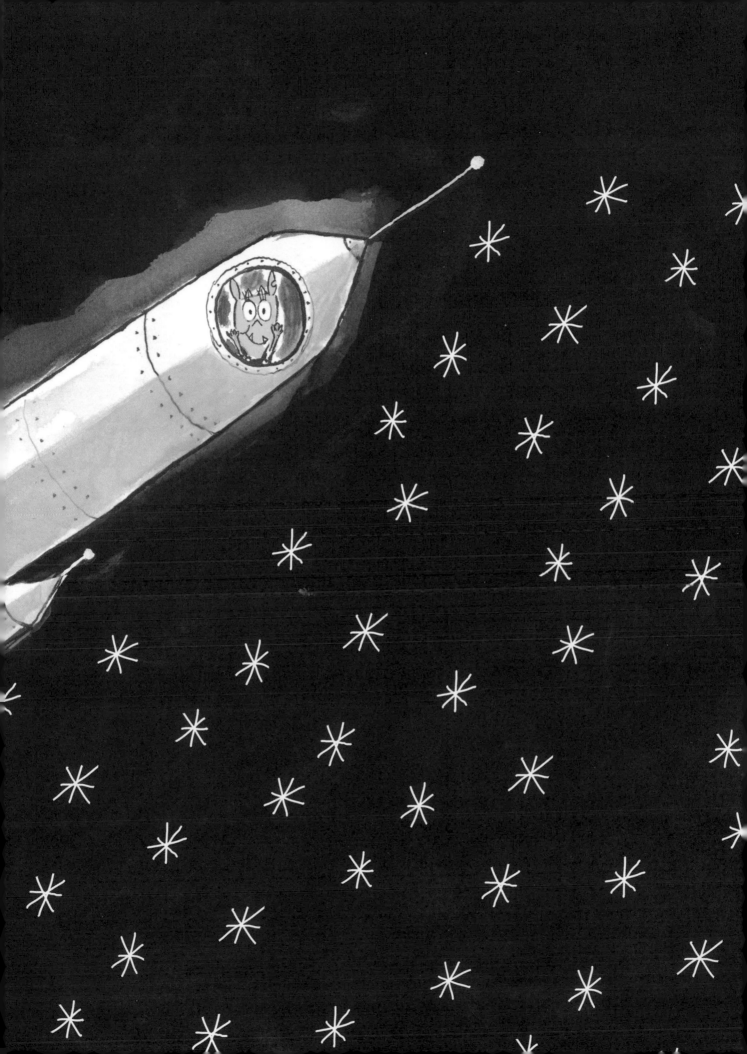

She is especially not allowed to catch a space alien that
spits acid. It would drool everywhere and ruin the floors.

Space creatures are awful monsters, and Ginny Goblin
cannot have a monster for a pet!

Not a giant monster or a fire-breathing monster or a petrifying monster or any kind of monster . . .

We can't let any of those pets into the house. Or the country. Or the planet. Do you think you can find a pet that isn't a monster?

What? You can? Okay then. What do you have in mind?

Look! Ginny Goblin has a baby goat. Goats don't crush things in their tentacles or set them on fire or petrify them or try to eat them. Goats even eat all the weeds in the yard. A baby goat is not a monster at all.

I think he'll be a great pet. Well done, Ginny Goblin.

Good work, everybody. Now let's take Ginny and her baby goat home. It's almost time for her to get ready for bed.

Wait a minute.

Didn't I say something about goats in the house?

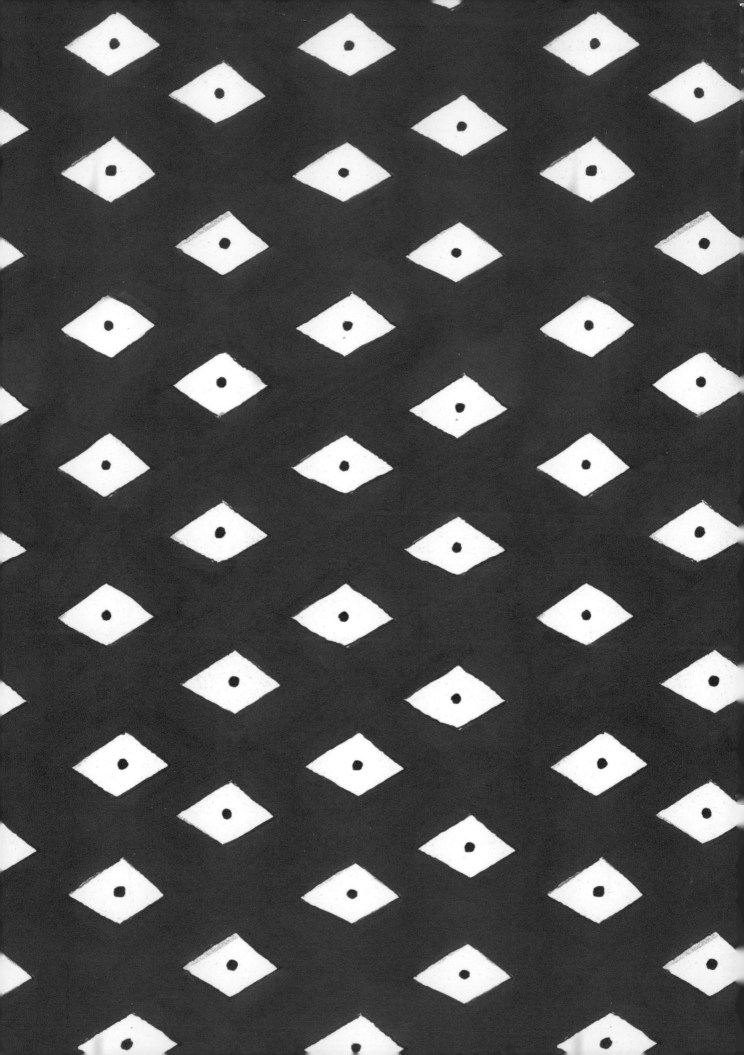